D1541230

To my mum, Ella Grey, and my dad, Peter Grey

Many thanks to KIM for consenting to a guest appearance.

The author and the publishers would like to thank the Reader's Digest Association, Ltd.,
for permission to reprint an extract from the *Encyclopedia of Garden Plants and Flowers* © 1997.

Visit us on the Web! www.randomhouse.com/kids

Educators and librarians, for a variety of teaching tools, visit us at
www.randomhouse.com/teachers

The Library of Congress has cataloged the hardcover edition of this work as follows:

Grey, Mini.
The very smart pea and the princess-to-be / by Mini Grey.
p.   cm.
Summary: The pea gives its own version of what happened in the fairy tale "The Princess and the Pea,"
from the time of its birth in the Palace Garden until it helps arrange a royal marriage.
ISBN 978-0-375-82626-9 (trade) — ISBN 978-0-375-92626-6 (lib. bdg.)
[1. Peas—Fiction. 2. Princesses—Fiction.] I. Title.
PZ7.G873 Ve 2003 [E]—dc21 2002152879

ISBN 978-0-375-87370-6 (pbk.)

MANUFACTURED IN CHINA

10 9 8 7 6 5 4 3 2 1

First Dragonfly Books Edition 2011

The
VERY SMART PEA
and the
PRINCESS-TO-BE

MiNi GREY

DRAGONFLY BOOKS ⸺ NEW YORK

Many years ago, I was born in the Palace Garden, among rows of carrots and beets and cabbages.

I nestled snugly in a velvety pod with my brothers and sisters.
I felt a tingle. I knew that somehow I would be important.

WAYS WITH PEAS

Pea and Raspberry Jelly

Ingredients:

Fresh Peas
Butter
Raspberr

Method
Shell p
boilin
Mak
b

WAYS W

Petits Pois Su

Ingredients:

Fresh Peas
Butter
Little Biscuits
Vanilla Ice-cream

Method:
ll the peas and simmer un
ding water. Add a knob
two scoops of ice-cr
op. Pour over the

The time came for us to go to the Palace Kitchen. We were shelled and put in a bowl. We were going to be part of a New Recipe. Then, suddenly, I was picked from the pile! I was put in a little box, with soft tissue to protect me from bruising. And I was taken by the Queen.

At this point in my story, I'm going to have to give you some background information. Let's start with the Queen.

A year earlier, before I even started to grow on my pea plant, the Queen had been nagging her son. "You are nearly thirty-four years old, Prince!" she said. "It really is high time you married. The Public expects it. Your Kingdom demands it. And if you are not married within one year, I shall stop your allowance."

The Prince got quite a large allowance, and he really didn't want it to be taken away.

"I'll start looking for a bride immediately, Mother," he answered.

And the search began.

The Prince traveled the Known World. He met princesses of all shapes and sizes, with a wide range of hobbies and interests.

too grumpy

too sleepy

too pink

too scary

strange pets

But none of them seemed like a Real Princess.
Somehow they were not right for him.

After a year's search, the Prince returned home, feeling glum. "THAT'S ENOUGH!" shouted the Queen. She stormed off to the Palace Kitchen. She came back with me. In my little box. "Now," said the Queen, "listen carefully. This is something only queens know.

'A Real Princess will be able to feel this little pea as she sleeps, even if she is sleeping on top of twenty mattresses and feather beds. And you are going to marry the first girl who can feel this pea!"

The Globe

WANTED

A REAL Princess

varieties require 11 weeks from sowing to Sow seeds in trays or ... of seed compost in March ... transplant the seedlings to ... prepared plot. Grow ... on peas in single rows, ... 9–12 in. between plants ... sorting each with a bamboo ... out the tendrils and tie ... ant to its cane. Allow only ... ng shoot to develop and ... f all side-shoots as they appear.

... allow the flowers to set until ... before the date of the show, ... ch out the growing tip when ... vers have set on each plant. ... flowers open, spray with ... cide to prevent pea thrips. ... in a liquid feed once a ... ght. When cutting exhibition ... handle them by ... stem only.

... k the pods as soon ... ney are ready; cropping ... be reduced if ripe pods ... left unpicked.

When a row has finished cropping cut the haulms and add them to the compost heap; leave the roots in the ground to enrich it with nitrogen.

pests

APHIDS infest young shoots and leaves, causing a check to growth, and making the plants sticky and sooty.

Germinating seeds may be eaten by MILLIPEDES, and MICE may eat the seeds in the ground before they have a chance to germinate.

Caterpillars of the PEA MOTH tunnel into maturing pods and feed on the ripening peas, making them maggoty and useless.

PEA THRIPS sometimes appear in large numbers and produce a characteristic silvering of developing pods, as well as damaging flowers and leaves.

diseases

DAMPING-OFF may cause early-sown peas to rot.

DOWNY MILDEW shows as grey furry patches on the undersides of leaves

GREY MOULD attacks the s... pods in wet weather, cove... with a grey velvety fungal g... MANGANESE DEFICIENCY affec... producing dark rusty-re... inside, which are seen only... the pods are split open... POWDERY MILDEW produces... powdery coating on leav... stems.

root rot

ROOT ROT can be cause... different fungi, including... RHIZOCTONIA and BLAC... The roots die and often show... patches; the stem base... discoloured and may c... foliage turns yellow and... Diseased plants collapse.

VIRUS DISEASES cause vari... symptoms, such as... distortion of leaves; dea... the foliage; brown strea... and stems. They may also... DIE-BACK of shoots and... plants; the pods may be ro... ridged or distorted.

However do not be downhe... if your peas never... maturity; the pea is su... plant, and amply repays... and effort lavished upon... ... inty tendrils. ... well cov...

someday **your** princess **will** come

Months passed. I spent most nights in the darkness under a pile of twenty mattresses and feather beds and a princess.

In the morning, the Queen would ask,
"And how did you sleep, my dear?"
The princesses had been properly brought up.
They always answered politely:
"Like a log, thank you, Ma'am," or
"Like a baby, thank you, Ma'am,"
and they all said:
"WHAT a comfortable bed!"
They were, as I said, all very polite
princesses.
"The Prince will never find his
princess at this rate," I thought
to myself. "I must help.
Somehow."

One night, a furious storm raged.
Rain lashed the Palace. Thunderclaps shook the walls.
Lightning flashed through the window panes.
There was a little knock on the Palace door.
A small, wet person stood on the doormat.

"Could THIS be the Real Princess?" gasped the Queen.

Before she could say a word, the small,
wet person was put to bed on top
of the twenty mattresses and feather beds.
With me, of course, underneath.
In the darkness under the mattresses,
I recognized the soft snoring.
It was my gardener!
"I must help," I thought.
I tried jiggling and wriggling.
The snoring continued quietly.
"I must do something!" I thought.
I inched my way to the edge.
And then I started to climb. Slowly I
struggled to the top of the towering pile.
I softly rolled across the pillow, right to the
girl's ear. "There is something Large
and Round and very Uncomfortable in
the bed under you," I whispered.
And while she slept, I told her about
the Large Round Uncomfortable
thing for three hours.

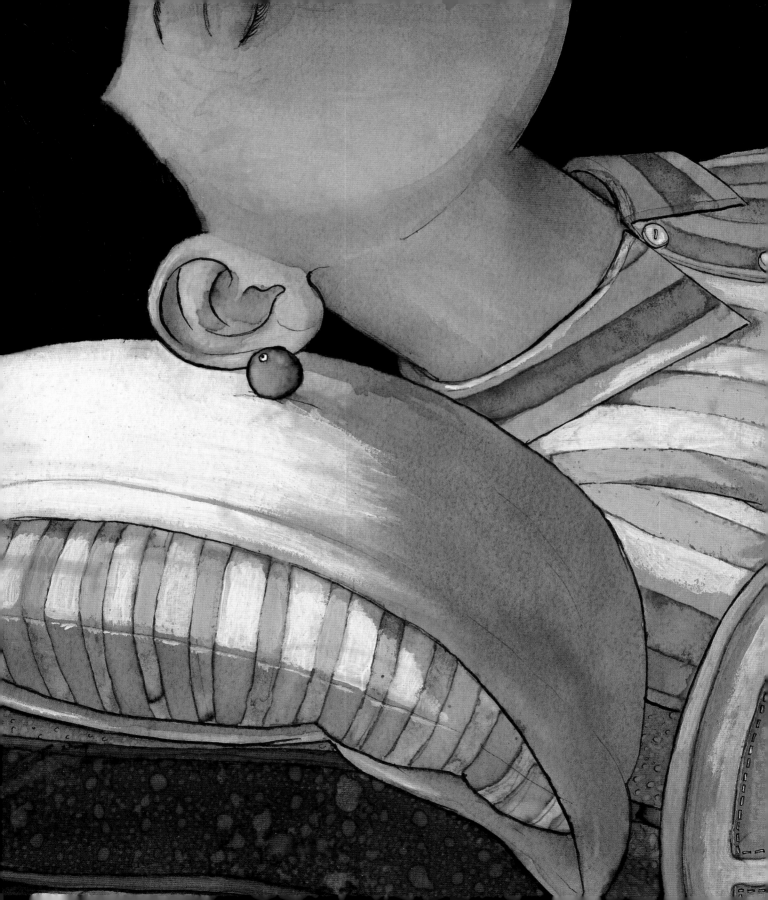

In the morning, the Queen asked
the girl how she had slept.
"Oh, it was awful!" she sighed.
"Something Large and Round and
Uncomfortable was bothering me
all night."
The Queen was delighted to
hear this.

The wedding was lovely.
The Queen was interested to meet the new Princess's parents.
And I'm sure they will all live together happily ever after.

And as for me? I became a Very Important Artifact.
And I now have my own glass case. I am On Display.
And if you visit the right museum and look in the right place,
you may chance to see me.

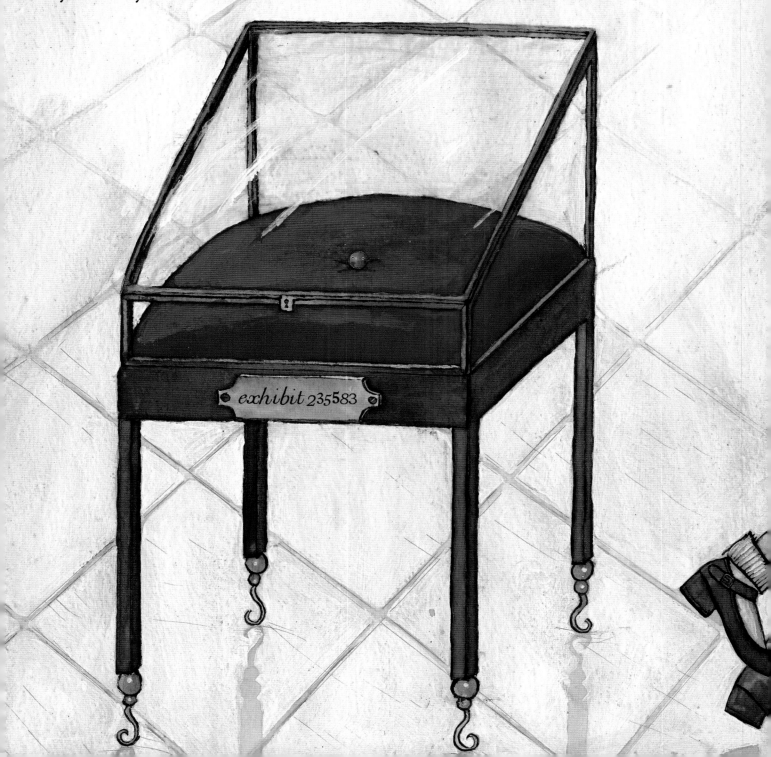

exhibit 235583

DRAGONFLY BOOKS

Dragonfly Books introduce children
to the pleasures of caring about and sharing books.
With Dragonfly Books, children will discover
talented artists and writers and
the worlds they have created,
ranging from first concept books to
read-together stories to books for
newly independent readers.

One of the best gifts a child can receive
is a book to read and enjoy.
Sharing reading with children today
benefits them now and in the future.

Begin building your child's future . . .
one Dragonfly Book at a time.

For help in selecting books your child will love, look for these themes on the back cover of every Dragonfly Book:

CLASSICS (Including Caldecott Award Winners)
CONCEPTS (Alphabet, Counting, and More)
CULTURAL DIVERSITY
DEATH AND DYING
FAMILY
FASCINATING PEOPLE
FRIENDSHIP
GROWING UP
JUST FOR FUN
MYTHS AND LEGENDS
NATURE AND OUR ENVIRONMENT
OUR HISTORY (Nonfiction and Historical Fiction)
POETRY
SCHOOL
SPORTS